THE DUMB BUNNIES
GO TO THE ZOO

by Dav Pilkey

THE BLUE SKY PRESS · AN IMPRINT OF SCHOLASTIC INC. · NEW YORK

For my nephews, Aaron and Connor Mancini

THE BLUE SKY PRESS

ISBN-13: 978-0-545-03937-6
ISBN-10: 0-545-03937-1

10 9 8 7 6 5 4 3 2 1   09 10 11 12 13

Printed in Singapore   46
This edition first printing, April 2009

The illustrations in this book were done with watercolors,
acrylics, India ink, low-fat vanilla yogurt, creamed asparagus,
and Tang Instant Breakfast Drink.

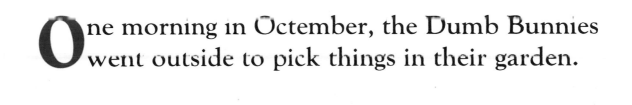

One morning in Octember, the Dumb Bunnies
went outside to pick things in their garden.

Momma Bunny was picking her flowers.

Poppa Bunny was picking his vegetables . . .

. . . and Baby Bunny was picking his nose.
"That's my boy!" said Poppa Bunny.

"What should we do today?" asked Momma Bunny.

"I want to go see paintings and sculptures and great works of art," said Baby Bunny.

"I know just the place," said Poppa Bunny.

So they headed off to the zoo.

When they got to the zoo, the Dumb Bunnies ran over to the ticket man.

"Duh, hi, lady," said Poppa Bunny.

"We'll take four tickets," said Momma Bunny.

"One for each of us," said Baby Bunny.

Inside the zoo, the Dumb Bunnies got
some ice cream and began to look around.

First they saw a tiny white creature standing on a sign.
"What's that animal?" asked Baby Bunny.
"Duh," said Poppa Bunny. "The sign says 'Elephant.'"
"I didn't know elephants had wings and feathers,"
said Momma Bunny.
"Me neither," said Poppa Bunny. "We sure are
learning a lot of things at the zoo."

ELEPHANT

Next they came to a cage and saw another tiny creature standing on a sign.

"What's that animal?" asked Baby Bunny.

"Duh," said Poppa Bunny. "The sign says 'Lion.'"

"That can't be a lion," said Momma Bunny.
"Lions have stripes!"
"You're right," said Poppa Bunny.

Suddenly, the strange creature fluttered off the sign and landed right on Momma Bunny's arm.
"Look, Momma," cried Baby Bunny. "It does have stripes!"

"Then it must be a LION!" screamed Momma Bunny.
"HELP! HELP! THE LION HAS ESCAPED!"

All at once the zoo was in a panic.
Everyone ran off screaming, "The lion is loose!"

Poppa and Baby Bunny ran to each of the animal cages
and opened the doors.

"THE LION IS LOOSE!" they screamed. "RUN FOR YOUR LIVES!" And the animals scattered in fear.

Soon, the police arrived to capture the dangerous lion.
"Where's the lion, ma'am?" asked the police chief.

"He flew away," said Momma Bunny.

After that, the Dumb Bunnies decided
it was time to go home.
"Weeeeee!" cried Baby Bunny.

On their way back to the parking lot, they came across two more strange creatures.

"What are those big animals?" asked Baby Bunny.

"Duh," said Poppa Bunny. "The box says 'Free Kitties.'"

"I wonder how much they cost?" asked Momma Bunny.

"Can I keep them?" asked Baby Bunny.
"All right," said Momma and Poppa Bunny.
"But only if you promise not to take care of them."
"I promise," said Baby Bunny.

Poppa Bunny tied Baby Bunny's new kitties
to the roof of the car.
"Duh, they'll be safe up here," he said.

The whole way home, Baby Bunny talked and talked about his new kitties.

"I sure do love my new kitties!" said Baby Bunny.
"I'm going to name them Pee-Pee and Wee-Wee."

Seconds later, the Dumb Bunnies pulled into their garage.
"The kitties are gone," said Poppa Bunny.
"Duh, what kitties?" asked Baby Bunny.

By now, it was getting late, so the Dumb Bunnies went inside and put on their new pajamas.

"I got these at a half-off sale!" said Momma Bunny.

"I thought so," said Poppa Bunny.

Then they crawled into their new water bed.
"This was the best week we've had all day,"
said Baby Bunny.
"That's my boy," said Poppa Bunny.

And as the sun set slowly in the East,
the Dumb Bunnies turned on all their lights,
said, "Good morning," and fell fast asleep.